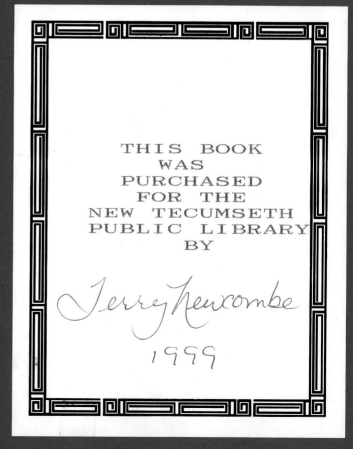

Baby Dreams

eugenie fernandes

Stoddart
Kids
TORONTO • NEW YORK

For
little Robyn Mari,
because I love you
more than spaghetti

*We acknowledge the Canada Council for the Arts and the
Ontario Arts Council for their support of our publishing program.*

Published in Canada in 1999 by
Stoddart Kids,
a division of Stoddart Publishing Co. Limited
34 Lesmill Road
Toronto, ON M3B 2T6
Tel (416) 445-3333 Fax (416) 445-5967
E-mail Customer.Service@ccmailgw.genpub.com

Published in the United States in 1999 by
Stoddart Kids,
a division of Stoddart Publishing Co. Limited
180 Varick Street, 9th Floor
New York, New York 10014
Toll free 1-800-805-1083
E-mail gdsinc@genpub.com

Distributed in Canada by
General Distribution Services
325 Humber College Blvd.,
Toronto, ON M9W 7C3
Tel (416) 213-1919 Fax (416) 213-1917
E-mail Customer.Service@ccmailgw.genpub.com

Distributed in the United States by
General Distribution Services
85 River Rock Drive, Suite 202
Buffalo, New York 14207
Toll free 1-800-805-1083
E-mail gdsinc@genpub.com

Canadian Cataloguing in Publication Data

Fernandes, Eugenie, 1943–
Baby dreams

ISBN 0-7737-3139-3

I. Title.

PS8561.E7596B32 1999   jC813'.54   C98-931797-8
PZ7.F47Ba 1999

*A mother wonders what dreams come to her sleeping baby,
and imagines different images while offering reassurance that
she will be there through the night.*

Printed and bound in Hong Kong
By Book Art Inc., Toronto

Foreword

I sit and watch the sunrise,
fleeting moments of gold and pink,
and I think about the world.

I think about babies . . .
easy to love.
Easy to forget they are watching us,
and listening.

We give them memories,
fleeting moments
that last forever.

e.f.

A lullaby of moonlight
sailing on the sea
rocks you to sleep,
Good night, Baby.

foreword

I sit and watch the sunrise,
fleeting moments of gold and pink,
and I think about the world.

I think about babies . . .
easy to love.
Easy to forget they are watching us,
and listening.

We give them memories,
fleeting moments
that last forever.

e.f.

A lullaby of moonlight
sailing on the sea
rocks you to sleep,
Good night, Baby.

Sweet dreams, I whisper.
And then
I wonder...
what do babies dream?

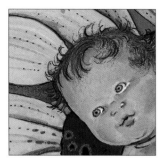

Maybe you dream
of a place far away
where babies play,
and colors fly.

Maybe a sky
with thunder crashing.
Raindrops falling.
Teardrops calling for a hug
to hold you safe
and warm.

Dream shadows dancing.
Little eyes watching . . .
I wonder what you see.

Maybe a face
and a smile
that is shining
just for you.

Blue water breezes blowing.
Toes wiggling in the sand.
Hands holding.
Babies splashing.

Little ears listening,
lost in a dream . . .
I wonder what you hear.

Far away echoes
and yesterday words.
You hear them all,
and you remember.

Suddenly you cry
in the middle of the night.
I wonder why . . .
but never mind.
Everything will be all right.
Sit with me a while.
Together
we can laugh at the dark.

Sleep again, Little one.
Dream.
And remember.
I will forever,
in sunlight or thunder,
be watching
and dreaming with you.